Old MacDonald Had a Farm

Illustrated by Carl and Mary Hauge

A GOLDEN BOOK • New York

Western Publishing Company, Inc., Racine, Wisconsin 53404

Old MacDonald had a farm,
Ee-igh, ee-igh, oh!
And on that farm he had some chicks,
Ee-igh, ee-igh, oh!
With a chick-chick here,
And a chick-chick there,
Here a chick, there a chick,
Everywhere a chick-chick.
Old MacDonald had a farm,
Ee-igh, ee-igh, oh!

And on that farm he had some horses,
Ee-igh, ee-igh, oh!
With a neigh-neigh here,
And a neigh-neigh there,
Here a neigh, there a neigh,
Everywhere a neigh-neigh.

And on that farm he had some turkeys,
Ee-igh, ee-igh, oh!
With a gobble-gobble here,
And a gobble-gobble there,
Here a gobble, there a gobble,
Everywhere a gobble-gobble.

And on that farm he had some ducks,
Ee-igh, ee-igh, oh!
With a quack-quack here,
And a quack-quack there,
Here a quack, there a quack,
Everywhere a quack-quack.

Old MacDonald had a farm,
Ee-igh, ee-igh, oh!
And on that farm he had some pigs,
Ee-igh, ee-igh, oh!

With an oink-oink here,
And an oink-oink there,
Here an oink, there an oink,
Everywhere an oink-oink.

And on that farm he had some cows,
Ee-igh, ee-igh, oh!
With a moo-moo here,
And a moo-moo there,
Here a moo, there a moo,
Everywhere a moo-moo.

And on that farm he had some dogs,
Ee-igh, ee-igh, oh!
With a bow-wow here,
And a bow-wow there,
Here a bow, there a wow,
Everywhere a bow-wow.

And on that farm he had some donkeys,
Ee-igh, ee-igh, oh!
With a hee-haw here,
And a hee-haw there,

Here a hee, there a haw,
Everywhere a hee-haw.
Old MacDonald had a farm,
Ee-igh, ee-igh, oh!

And on that farm he had some sheep,
Ee-igh, ee-igh, oh!
With a baa-baa here,

And a baa-baa there,
Here a baa, there a baa,
Everywhere a baa-baa.

With a hee-haw here,
And a hee-haw there,
Here a hee, there a haw,
Everywhere a hee-haw.

With a bow-wow here,
And a bow-wow there,
Here a bow, there a wow,
Everywhere a bow-wow.

With a moo-moo here,
And a moo-moo there,
Here a moo, there a moo,
Everywhere a moo-moo.

With an oink-oink here,
And an oink-oink there,
Here an oink, there an oink,
Everywhere an oink-oink.

With a quack-quack here,
And a quack-quack there,
Here a quack, there a quack,
Everywhere a quack-quack.

With a gobble-gobble here,
And a gobble-gobble there,
Here a gobble, there a gobble,
Everywhere a gobble-gobble.

With a neigh-neigh here,
And a neigh-neigh there,
Here a neigh, there a neigh,
Everywhere a neigh-neigh.

With a chick-chick here,
And a chick-chick there,
Here a chick, there a chick,
Everywhere a chick-chick.
Old MacDonald had a farm,
Ee-igh, ee-igh, oh!

Old MacDonald Had a Farm

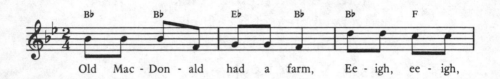

Old Mac - Don - ald had a farm, Ee - igh, ee - igh,

oh! And on that farm he had some chicks,

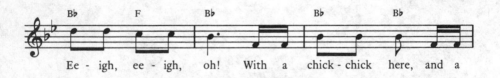

Ee - igh, ee - igh, oh! With a chick - chick here, and a

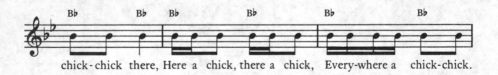

chick - chick there, Here a chick, there a chick, Every-where a chick-chick.

Old Mac - Don - ald had a farm, Ee - igh, ee - igh, oh!